# Archibald Mountbank
# and the
# Miniscule Miracles

# Archibald Mountbank and the Miniscule Miracles

## G.A. Milnthorpe

ROUNDFIRE
BOOKS

Winchester, UK
Washington, USA

JOHN HUNT PUBLISHING

First published by Roundfire Books, 2021
Roundfire Books is an imprint of John Hunt Publishing Ltd., No. 3 East St., Alresford,
Hampshire SO24 9EE, UK
office@jhpbooks.com
www.johnhuntpublishing.com
www.roundfire-books.com

For distributor details and how to order please visit the 'Ordering' section on our website.

Text copyright: G.A. Milnthorpe 2020

ISBN: 978 1 78904 917 6
978 1 78904 918 3 (ebook)
Library of Congress Control Number: 2021933143

A CIP catalogue record for this book is available from the British Library.

Design: Stuart Davies

UK: Printed and bound by CPI Group (UK) Ltd, Croydon, CR0 4YY
Printed in North America by CPI GPS partners

We operate a distinctive and ethical publishing philosophy in
all areas of our business, from our global network of authors to
production and worldwide distribution.

## Also by G.A. Milnthorpe

*Stanley Young is Planning a Murder in a Very Precise and Intricate Manner* (ISBN-10: 1909421235. ISBN-13: 978-1909421233)

*Second Hand Scott* (ISBN-10: 1782284397.
ISBN-13: 978-1782284390)

*Charlie Farley Pumpkin-Bum and the Case of the Disappearing Twin* (for children) (ISBN-10: 1081280824. ISBN-13: 978-1081280826)
Available from all the usual places.

Dedicated to my wife, Beck, and my children, Charlie and Poppy... if only I could be one per cent better as a husband and a father...

"The average person, in my estimation, is ninety-nine per cent animal and one per cent human. The ninety-nine per cent that is animal causes very little trouble."
Joseph Weil, American "conman", 1875–1976

Barnum statements: statements that in most cases apply to everyone, but always sound very specific to the individual. They are used by psychics, fortune tellers, horoscopes, mediums and the like to give the impression of insight.

# Chapter 1

# Security is one of your major goals in life

On my first morning with Archibald Mountbank, he welcomed a young, attractive girl into his office and, within a few moments, had his hairy hand between her huge breasts. The speed of the manoeuvre was remarkable. Just seconds before, she had been sobbing and he had been stroking the back of her hand.

"Go on, if you can," Mountbank said in his gentle voice. "Take your time."

"Mr Mountbank, you're so kind," the girl said. She dabbed at her eyes with her free hand.

"I just want to help you."

He continued to stroke her hand; soothing her, calming her. The sobs gently subsided. He stroked the back of her hand with the back of his; the dark hairs on his knuckles lightly brushing her young, firm, milky white skin.

She had been quite business-like when she walked into Mountbank's consulting room. Dark, well-fitted clothing. Bright red lipstick – stark against her pale face. A phone in one hand, car keys in the other. I found myself wondering what she did for a living... accountant, human resources, lawyer? She had bustled in, nodding to the Ever-Present Ogden in his corner and also to me in mine.

"Good morning Mr Mountbank, thank you for seeing me..."

She thrust out her hand, maintaining the edifice of a business-like encounter.

But she had crumbled quickly.

I soon discovered that she had walked into that room in the same way that most people walk in – with an air of busy scepticism that seemed to say *what the hell am I doing here?* and *let's make this quick shall we?* Quite a few of those sceptics were crying within the first minute too.

"When you're ready…" said Mountbank.

"I don't love my husband," she said at last. "But I want to."

Mountbank continued to stroke. And stare. Unless his eyes were closed, they were staring.

"He's a nice man. Kind and sweet. Attentive. Interesting. All the things you'd put in a lonely-hearts column. But I don't love him. I don't suppose I ever have."

"That is terribly sad," said Mountbank, in his quiet little voice. Even from my corner of his consulting room, barely three metres away, I had to strain to catch his gentle words. The girl must have been struggling too because she leaned forward. "Marriage is a sacred institution. The marriage vow is hallowed. It is not to be spurned lightly."

"I know," said the girl.

"Have you considered leaving him?"

"Yes, but I can't. We're married, like you said. And he's… he's nice. I don't know how else to describe him. He's just nice. I don't want to hurt him. And besides, divorce is just so complicated. My parents would be devastated. They really do love him. The sun shines out of his… never mind. All our friends… the house… our cat… everything… it's just too much. Everything would have to change. No, it's better that I stay with him. Give it a go. Make it work. That's why I'm here."

Mountbank nodded as if he understood the dilemma. Perhaps he did. I had met his wife.

"And what would you like me to do?" asked Mountbank.

"I was hoping you could help me. Help me love him more. Just a little."

Mountbank seemed to consider this, as if the request was some sort of surprise. As if he hadn't been encountering ridiculous aspirations like that for the last however many years.

"May I ask you a personal question?" he asked, once he had got over his self-imposed shock.

2

"Of course."

"Is there someone else? Another man? Or woman?"

The pretty, young girl withdrew her hand from Mountbank's palm and crossed her arms. That was an answer in itself.

"Yes," she said after a moment, having cast a quick glance at Ogden and one at me. It occurred to me that she might be uncomfortable with that line of questioning in the presence of three men – one of whom was taking notes. "A man."

"And you're sleeping with him?"

"Yes."

"Frequently?"

"Yes."

"Where?" asked Mountbank.

"Where?" she asked.

"Yes, where?"

"Is that relevant?" asked the young girl.

For the record – it wasn't relevant.

"If you want me to help you," said Mountbank, "it is important that you are completely honest with me – even if that includes details of an intimate nature. If we are to grow, we must firstly survey the soil in which we stand."

I wrote that down. *If we are to grow...* My editor would love that kind of claptrap. She could recycle it as part of a self-help manual to follow the release of my book. A lovely hardback tome full of meaningless slogans like that; the kind of book sold at a heavily discounted price in the run-up to Christmas. I could imagine T-shirts and aprons too. *The Mountbank Method. Live Your Life the Mountbank Way.* It did amaze me that Mountbank hadn't started diversifying his bullshit. Mugs, calendars, bookmarks, he could have cashed in. Why hadn't he? Money grabbing swine. And, more to the point, why hadn't Ogden leveraged these revenue streams? That was all that Ogden was interested in – money. And other people's wives. I wondered what kind of soil Ogden was in.

However, it had the desired effect on the pretty girl. It almost always did. She told Mountbank about the soil... the dirty soil beneath her feet.

"We meet in a hotel once or twice a week, depending on when we can both get away."

"And you have... sex?"

He said the word as if it were distasteful to him. Or as if it were something he couldn't quite comprehend. Both might have been true. As I've said, I had met his wife.

"Yes. Mostly."

"Once? Twice?"

The girl hesitated... but then thought again of the soil in which she was standing. Sinking even.

"Sometimes twice," she said. "But it's not just sex..."

Mountbank closed his eyes and leaned back into his chair, stopping the girl in her self-justifying tracks. He didn't move. I couldn't even hear him breathing. The room was unnervingly quiet. The pretty girl looked at Ogden, but he was sitting in his corner, flicking through his phone as always. She looked at me but I just shrugged. I had just as much idea about what was going on as she did – none. We both continued to watch Mountbank as he... what? I don't know... reclined. Meditated? Prayed? Dissembled?

"You don't love him? Your husband?" Mountbank asked eventually, breaking the awkward silence. The girl and I both jumped a little. Mountbank still had his eyes closed.

"No."

"Not even a little?"

"I don't think so."

"In which case I can't help you. You can't increase what doesn't exist. That is beyond even my power."

The pretty girl started to sob again. It is no exaggeration to say that her bosom heaved. Perhaps that's why Mountbank was sorry.

"I'm so sorry. You've driven all this way," said Mountbank as he re-opened his eyes, re-took her hand and re-commenced the stroking of her soft skin.

"Isn't there *anything* you can do?" asked the girl, between snotty sobs.

He thought for a moment, as if he were working through some complicated mathematical sum. He seemed to be staring off into the middle distance. From my seat in the corner I couldn't be sure, but I wondered if the middle distance might be somewhere around the pretty girl's breasts.

"I suppose I could increase your capacity for love. It is possible. But it would then be up to you to fill that capacity from the right source, from your husband. The danger would be that you simply end up increasing your attachment to this man who uses your body two or three times a week."

The pretty girl stiffened, perhaps offended by Mountbank's choice of words, or perhaps by the way he had said them. But she didn't remove her hand this time. She bit her lip.

"I'd like to try."

"In which case, I'm afraid we approach the rather indelicate part..."

He tailed off, as if this were also distasteful to him. Or, like the sex, something that he couldn't quite comprehend... which was nonsense given his estimated net worth.

"I have money. How much is it?"

"We do not charge a fee," said Mountbank.

"But I thought...?"

Everyone knew there was a cost. That's why people hated him, once they'd stopped loving him.

"There is no fee. But if you would care to make a donation, I would be most appreciative."

"Okay. So how much do you want me to donate?"

"For you, today, one hundred pounds. If you want to, of course."

The girl heaved a sigh of relief. She'd probably heard the stories of it costing a whole lot more. Rumour had it that the British Army had paid, sorry *donated*, millions for a consultation in the 1990s. They had denied it of course. My editor particularly wanted me to dig into that one.

"If you could just see my associate..."

Mountbank directed the pretty girl towards Ogden with a flourish of his hairy hand.

Short and bulky with a shaved head and an expensive suit, Ogden looked more like a nightclub bouncer than the Commercial Manager to one of the nation's richest men. He looked instantly dislikeable and I knew, from personal experience, that this first impression was the right one.

I found it difficult to be in the same room as him.

"Can I pay on card?" asked the girl.

"I'd prefer cash," said Ogden.

Once Ogden had pocketed the cash, for which no receipt was given, the pretty girl returned her attention to Mountbank, only to find him with his eyes closed once more. Ogden returned to his phone, not caring to explain or otherwise reassure, leaving me and the girl to look at Mountbank's eyelids again. I offered another shrug.

I soon came to realise that Mountbank closed his eyes a lot. In any brief moment of respite during his day he would be found with his eyes closed. At first I wondered if he might be narcoleptic. And then I wondered if he might just need to give his eyes a break from all that intense staring. Or perhaps it was just because he was quite old.

"Is he meditating?" I asked Ogden, a few weeks in.

"How the hell should I bloody know?" he had replied with his usual charm and tact.

"Close your eyes," said Mountbank to the girl, having just opened his.

She did.

"Clear your mind. Clear your mind of this man and his lust for you. Be at peace."

Mountbank placed his furry hand between her breasts. I wrote that down. In fact, I wrote that Mountbank has put his hands between her big breasts... because they were. I had to write that. My editor would want to know that. She would want that in the book.

"The capacity for love is not found within the heart. It is simply a pump for circulating blood around the body. However, as a spiritual approximation it will serve well."

She waited. We waited. No one said a word. Mountbank kept his hand pressed against the girl's chest. For a wonder, he didn't close his eyes. He just stared at her for what seemed like a very, very long time.

"It is done."

Mountbank removed his hand and sat back in his chair. He heaved an exhausted sigh. There was sweat upon his brow. His eyes, framed by huge spectacles, were redder than before. He looked strained. But from what, I wondered.

"Is that it?" asked the pretty girl.

"Indeed."

"I don't feel any different."

"You will. In time. That small increase will become apparent as you search within."

"What does that mean?"

Mountbank closed his eyes again. He looked spent.

"I don't understand – have you increased my capacity for love or not? I don't feel any different."

Ogden spoke: "Mrs Barrett, I'm afraid your time is up."

"But..." she tried.

"Your time is up," interrupted Ogden. "Mr Mountbank is very tired after your consultation. If you wouldn't mind stepping out into the waiting room...?"

As Ogden saw Mrs Barrett to the door, guiding her unerringly with his stocky frame that brooked no argument, I found myself wanting to ask a question, but Mountbank had his eyes closed again and Ogden had told me – in no uncertain terms – that I wasn't to speak to Mountbank alone. Terms of the deal.

So we sat in silence.

When Ogden returned, he was angry. He barrelled into the room, banging the door.

"You're supposed to ask, you bloody idiot," he snapped.

Mountbank, eyes closed, said in his gentle voice: "Pardon?"

"Before you put hands on them, you're supposed to ask. You have to get consent. You know that."

"I forgot."

"Tell that to the police when they drag you in again and take a sample. You forgot. Bloody idiot. They warned you…"

"I didn't do anything," said Mountbank. He opened his eyes and looked genuinely insulted – hurt even. A bit scared maybe. In that moment, with the irate, heavyset figure of Ogden leering above him, I actually felt sorry for Mountbank. A bit.

He looked old, worn out. Knackered. Spent.

He hadn't looked like that when he had his hand placed between that girl's breasts, so my sympathy passed.

Postscript – a few months after her consultation with Mountbank, I was able to track down the pretty girl, Mrs Barrett, and get an update on her marital situation. She had left her husband.

## Chapter 2

# You have a great deal of unused capacity which you have not turned to your advantage

Mountbank started to stand... pushing up slowly from his padded chair. I heard a click as he did, perhaps from a knee or a hip. It's funny how a man can instantly age when he stands or sits. He looked fully his seventy-two years of age.

"Where you going?" asked Ogden, in his best mockney accent. "Sit down."

At the sound of Ogden's voice, Mountbank froze, caught in mid-crouch.

"It's after five," he said from his semi-vertical position.

"So?"

I glanced at my watch. It was after five, three minutes beyond. I had only been with Mountbank for a few days and I knew that he never went beyond five o' clock. Very much a creature of habit. Start at 9am, lunch between 1pm and 2pm, finish at 5pm. There was coffee and a biscuit at 10.30am. A tea and biscuit at 2.30pm. A solitary toilet break at 11.30am. Each appointment scheduled for thirty minutes. All strictly enforced. I imagined that his home life must be the same... *It's the third Thursday of the month dear, I suppose we should do the deed...*

"Is someone still outside?" asked Mountbank. "It's after five."

"Yes, there is someone outside."

"Who? It's after five."

"Money. A big walking bag of money pressed into an Armani suit."

"But it's after five."

"It will only take a minute."

"But it's after five."

Ogden snorted. "Cash cows don't stick to office hours. I'll bring him in. Sit down."

Ogden ignored a further weak call of "it's after five" and headed out to the waiting room. As the door closed, Mountbank gave himself up to gravity and flopped back onto the padded chair. He didn't groan, but I thought I could see a tremble in his leg – perhaps from too much exertion in his thigh muscles, or that troublesome knee that I had imagined. I tried to catch Mountbank's eye, to see if I could get a glimpse of what he really thought of Ogden – a raised eyebrow or a roll of the eyes – but he wouldn't look at me. Not for the first time, I wondered how this unlikely pair had become business partners. Mountbank had survived for years, decades, without any sort of agent or manager or handler; through all the peak years of his notoriety and money-making prowess. He hadn't needed any commercial management whilst he was making his millions and being sued left, right and centre. But then suddenly, five years before, Ogden had somehow got involved, passing round his business card that said,

Harry Ogden, Esq.

Commercial Manager to Archibald Mountbank.

My editor was keen for that side of the story too, particularly given Ogden's history. But I imagine Ogden had told Mountbank the same thing that he had told me – no chat without Ogden himself being present. All conversation to be chaperoned.

A few seconds later, Ogden was back, followed by an attractive, expensive looking man. From his shiny shoes to his old school tie, it was immediately obvious that this man had money. He had an aura that only the outrageously rich seem to have; making me immediately feel self-conscious about my open necked shirt and brown shoes. He even made Ogden, who seemed to apply almost all of his disposable income towards tailored suits and pungent aftershave, look a bit second-rate.

As he stepped into the consulting room and looked around, the expensive man said, sarcastically, "No expense spared I see..."

Mountbank, for a wonder, had his eyes open.

"It serves," said Mountbank. "Please take a seat."

The man took a seat. Or rather, the seat. It was a cheap seat in a cheap room; the expensive man was right about that. A blank room. No cupboards. No cabinets. No pictures, no photographs, no inspirational quotes etched onto the wall. Just four cheap plastic chairs and a low table with a water jug on it. Mountbank was the only one with padding on his chair – an accommodation to his age, I suppose.

Two months before I was admitted into the presence of the elusive Mountbank, the police had raided his office. Some disgruntled former customer, dissatisfied with his treatment and sore about the £10,000 he had paid for it, had told the police that Mountbank was hoarding enough pharmaceuticals in his office to open a small dispensary. The tip-off claimed that Mountbank would dole out drugs to his patients in an entirely un-medical way.

The police stormed the office in a polite and gentle way, knocking before entering and calling Mr and Mrs Mountbank, "sir" and "madam." Very British. But then they tore the place apart. They found nothing. Literally nothing. No records, no files, no computers, and certainly no drugs. The fact that the office was so bare had only heightened their suspicions. They searched everywhere... above the suspended ceiling, under the floorboards, in the toilet cistern... everywhere they could think of. They even patted down Ogden as he had that air of criminality about him, but he just smirked. They found absolutely nothing. The police officer who told me about it was still pissed...

"A bloke like that shouldn't have an office like that... it's weird. There's got to be more to it..."

The man in the tailored suit may have been thinking the

same, and he also had that familiar look on his face... *What the hell am I doing here...?* but he didn't look the type to crumble into tears, nor the type to let Mountbank stroke him with his hairy hand. He looked at Mountbank with some amusement, perhaps at the sheer anti-climax of meeting him. I had done the same, I think, when I first met him. He looked smaller and older in real life. The newspaper shots, always from a distance, and the court sketches, exaggerated him somehow... always showing him at some sinister angle.

Mountbank was wearing a green V-neck jumper that, whilst neat, had no veneer of reassuring expense. His trousers had no hint of a pinstripe. And his shoes had a velveteen texture and could have doubled as carpet slippers. His socks were plain and his glasses were many decades behind trend. It was not hard to imagine Mountbank wearing the same clothes – the very same – in his former life, before the millions and the fame and the lawsuits. Much like the consulting room itself, Mountbank was... functional. No expense spent indeed.

"How can I help you?" Mountbank asked in his gentle voice.

The man in the suit didn't mess around with pleasantries.

"I want you to increase my stock holdings by one per cent."

"That I can't do."

The man looked at Ogden, for an answer or an explanation or an intervention. Ogden did look like the boss, what with his suits and his scent and the gaudy rings on both hands, including a ridiculous looking sovereign on his thumb. Many a client would step into the office and assume that Ogden was actually the famous Archibald Mountbank, miracle worker, mystical healer, spiritual improver. And if not that, many seemed to assume that Ogden was in charge – like the nicely dressed pimp standing in the shadows. The organ grinder to Mountbank's monkey.

"What is this? I was told he could increase anything. He came highly recommended."

Mountbank answered.

"I can only deal with real things – tangible, physical. I need to be able to touch, to feel, to find the deficiency within your soul. Anything that exists within the digital ether, I cannot touch, therefore I cannot change."

The man sighed – irritated, exasperated.

I bit my tongue... I wouldn't have described a capacity to love – the gift he had bestowed on the girl with the big breasts just a few days before – as being tangible. What a bloody liar.

"I've wasted a whole day. For this crap. You're a conman."

Mountbank closed his eyes once more, not even tempted to respond to the man in the suit. He'd heard the accusation before, many times. It had been shouted in the streets, through car windows and across parks. It had been written in countless letters, some demanding money and some predicting his death. He'd seen it as newspaper headlines which had become increasingly vitriolic as the years went by. He'd seen it in court papers. He'd even seen it in the Radio Times. Conman. Charlatan. Fraud.

The man in the suit stood and looked like he was on the verge of hitting Mountbank, or at least pulling some of the remaining strands of hair out of his head. I don't think he liked being told "no".

"I've been here all bloody day."

He turned to go.

"I'm sure there's something Mr Mountbank could do to help you," said Ogden, in a rare interjection. "Isn't there?"

Mountbank opened his eyes and seemed to think for a while.

He did a lot of thinking, did Mountbank. He reminded me of a plumber inhaling and saying "this will cost you..."

"I could increase your capacity for wisdom I suppose. Or perhaps increase your level of discernment?"

I didn't bother to write that down. I'd only been with Mountbank for a few days and he had been increasing capacity left, right and centre. Capacity for love, capacity for empathy, capacity for self-control... anything abstract it seemed to me. Today was the first time I'd heard the word "tangible".

On my second day with Mountbank, a similarly rich man had entered the consulting room and asked Mountbank to smooth out the surface of his private grass tennis court. I thought it was a joke at first but when I looked round the room, no one seemed to be laughing.

"It's not bad, I've had professionals in, but there are some areas of uneven bounce. If you could help..."

Mountbank had taken £10,000 from that man, and hadn't spoken about the need to "touch the tangible" or "feel what is real". The rich man had asked if Mountbank needed to see the court or apply his hands to the grass but Mountbank had declined. It seemed he could work his magic remotely, when the situation demanded it.

"You're selling me something I don't need," said the man in the suit, "You don't sell ice to the eskimos and you don't sell business acumen to me. Don't you even know who I am?"

I did, obviously. But he wouldn't let me say. Not in print – not when he found out about the book. I got a very nice letter from his lawyer.

Mountbank smiled, "I don't see much of the outside world."

"Obviously."

The man headed for the door but hesitated before he reached the handle. "How much would it cost? This increase in my discernment?"

"One million pounds," said Mountbank simply.

I flinched... there had been rumours about Mountbank and his money-making potential, but to hear it confirmed... Ogden didn't blink an eyelid. He was back on his phone... probably texting other people's wives.

The rich man laughed.

"A million? You're out of your mind."

"If you are to gain the benefit of my abilities, you must invest in it. You cannot offer a sacrifice that costs you nothing. Are you familiar with the story of the widow's mite in the Bible?"

I didn't write that down either. He had a startling lack of variation in his patter. The soil of growth. The widow's mite. Looking backwards to look forwards. Searching within to look without. The eye of a needle. Driving a camel. Much of it seemed to come from his church days. I wondered how Ogden could stand it.

"Yes, yes, heard that one, poor little widow. Look, don't give me any religious hocus pocus, or any of your voodoo crap. I'm being shafted. You're shafting me. You know it. I know it – don't try and dress it up. Half a million and we have a deal."

"I don't parley. You either want it or you don't."

The man grinned, showing some genuine good humour for the first time since he entered the room. "I quite like you Mr Mountbank. I wish I employed you. You know people."

"How do you mean?"

"You can see I'm a greedy bastard so you know I'll pay. It was just a case of naming your price. Come on then, let's get this done."

I wrote that down. It was a good observation. Mountbank certainly knew his audience, particularly those falling within the *more money than sense* demographic.

Mountbank stood and placed a hairy hand on the man's stomach; low down, near his groin.

"Our capacity for wisdom isn't found within the gut, but as a physical approximation it will serve..."

Postscript – Just before going to press, the latest Sunday Times Rich List revealed that the man in the suit had jumped up two places, having increased his personal wealth by six per cent. He'd bought when others were selling, apparently.

And I managed to get in touch with the man with the tennis court. He said the surface did seem to be delivering a "surer bounce."

## Chapter 3

# While you have some personality weaknesses, you are generally able to compensate for them

The people who enter Mountbank's consulting room are entirely random. Randomly chosen I should say. But also random in the other sense of the word. You never quite know who might walk through that door. It might be a terminally ill octogenarian wanting an extra one per cent of health to prolong her life; or an amateur boxer wanting a slightly bigger bicep to improve his career prospects in the ring. It might be a university undergraduate wanting a bigger brain, or a middle-aged divorcee wanting a bigger bust.

Greed, tragedy and desperation – they entered the room on a loose rotation.

When Mountbank first opened his office, after a few years of freelancing in the back seat of his car, he would see anyone, strictly on a first-come-first-served basis. He issued tickets, not unlike raffle tickets, to keep order. Even on day one, when he hadn't yet featured in a television documentary or been investigated by Trading Standards, he had quite a following... from his days in the church probably. The circumstances of his ejection from the faith must have spread like wildfire through those evangelical grapevines. Many of them were waiting outside his door on his first day as a *consultant* – having heard about his healing hands.

As his popularity grew, and as people started flocking from the world over, drawn in ever increasing numbers by the scandal and the intrigue and the reports of success, he stayed true to his principles – issuing slightly more professional looking tickets and telling people to wait their turn. One out, one in.

There is no charge for a ticket.

Mountbank's office is in a small commercial development between a train station and a river. On the door it simply says, Archibald Mountbank: Consultant. There is a pub behind and a rough car park in front. He's in Unit 3. The other two are filled by an accountant and a physiotherapist. I once tried a joke with Mountbank... that he'd somehow managed to combine those two professions – healing hands and money management – into one... but he didn't laugh. When Ogden found out about it, he said:

"Mountbank doesn't do jokes, you dickhead."

Only two patients are allowed in the building at any one time. One in the consultation room, with Mountbank and his hairy hands, and another in the waiting room with Mrs Mountbank and her floral blouses. As for the others, they wait outside, although they aren't supposed to, due to complaints from the other tenants who found their designated car parking spaces perpetually occupied by desperate loiterers.

Instead, the patients – or petitioners – or clients, are supposed to keep an eye on his very basic website (manually updated by his wife) which tells them the ticket/appointment number that Mountbank has reached. When their number gets close, they should make their arrangements for attending the appointment. And don't miss it... otherwise you go to the back of the queue. No excuses, no deferrals, no notes from your doctor or your mum, no blaming the trains or the traffic. If you're three minutes late you might as well just go home and start waiting again.

His current waiting list is 3919 tickets long. As he sees an average of 14 people per day, the person at the end of the line has a good year to wait.

The car park, despite the warnings from Mountbank's landlord, was always full to the brim of suitors – the worried, the desperate and the vain. They ignored the signs telling them that parking was prohibited. They ignored the dirty looks from the accountant and the physiotherapist. They ignored the fact that their ticket wouldn't get them through the door for months yet. It is no exaggeration to say that people would wait weeks, just on the off-chance of seeing Mountbank. They would live in their cars, or pitch a tent for as long as they could get away with it, or simply wait in line, just hoping... always hoping.

Some intrepid petitioners would try to harangue Mountbank as he entered or left the office, trying to get some of his attention. But it did no good. Mountbank kept his eyes down.

Every now and then, Mountbank would have a no-show – quite possibly one of those people holding onto a ticket with one hand but also holding back a terminal disease with the other, or perhaps someone whose cynicism just got the better of them – and in that event, the highest placed ticket in the car park or queuing outside the door would be substituted in.

The system was rigid.

Ticket number 1824, come in please...

Mountbank showed no favour, not even to those on the brink of death, although he often said (when he was eventually allowed to speak to me) that one per cent could be the difference between survival and extinction. Just one touch of his healing hands could give someone another Christmas, or could nurse them through a wedding day, or give them enough time to see a new-born baby. It might even be just enough to tip them into remission, or to ward off a stroke or heart failure. But Mountbank wouldn't change his system, even in the face of heartbreak. Everyone had to wait their turn.

"Everyone who comes into this room has a matter of life and death to contend with," he said. "For some, it just happens to be a physical death..."

I wrote that down, even though it was clearly bollocks.

The man charged with Mountbank's security, a brute of a man called Adam, told me that the car park was fuller than usual of late... owing to the rumours of Mountbank's impending retirement.

The rumours were true, hence why Ogden had accepted my phone call, my offer and my money. Well, the publisher's money. People wanted to get to Mountbank before he retired from public life. The limitless potential in Mountbank's hands was suddenly limited. It created a small panic. So, they waited, these car park squatters, hoping to be selected in the event of someone else's untimely death or other misfortune.

I had my suspicions about just how random the selection of substitutes was... given that it was Ogden who would venture out into the car park to find a replacement for the no-show. Mrs Mountbank dutifully issued tickets to anyone who wanted one – whether prince or pauper – but it was Ogden who was responsible for filling the occasional gaps in Mountbank's schedule. He was the one who watched the clock, waiting for it to click to three minutes past the appointed time.

"Time's up," he'd say as he headed into the car park, rubbing his hands.

And that replacement would somehow always seem to be someone of significant means. Ogden would roll his eyes every time Mountbank charged ten pounds to improve an old lady's eyesight, or even a hundred pounds to strengthen a semi-professional footballer's knee ligament. And lo... whenever Ogden went on a trawl of the car park, he always somehow managed to find someone of high net worth, or at least someone with an ability to quickly access significant amounts of credit. Ogden smirked when I asked him about it... but he didn't say anything.

Smarmy bastard.

Mountbank didn't seem to care. He just saw whoever came through the door – touching whoever fate, or Ogden, brought to him. It didn't seem to matter to him whether he was dealing with someone with a brain tumour or someone with male pattern baldness.

"And what seems to be the problem today? Acne...?"

Whilst his speciality was increasing internal capacities – courage, wisdom, determination – he wasn't averse to strengthening the body. He would add one per cent to the hair on a man's head, he would expand a girl's breasts or increase a man's height. I was amazed at just how many short men came to visit Mountbank. I would guess they outnumbered the sick and the dying by two to one at least. And rumour had it that any number of professional sportsmen and women had been to visit him, with a view to gaining a one per cent increase in their red blood cells or increased lung capacity. (Not that I could actually get any of them to admit to it.)

I asked Ogden one day: "do you have any files that I could look at?"

"No."

"No list of clients?"

"No. We're discreet. Anyway, they're not clients, strictly speaking."

"What about evidence? Measurements? Proof? Didn't you compile something for one of the court cases?"

"Might have. Can't remember."

"You must have something for tax purposes?"

"Maybe I do. But that's for me to know and you to find out."

Dickhead. He used to say that at school.

One day, perhaps in my third week with Mountbank, a pale, shaven haired man placed his huge penis on the table next to the water jug. Mountbank had his eyes closed as the man entered and nearly jumped out of his chair when he opened them to see the gargantuan yet still flaccid member before him. Whether he was shocked at the size of the thing or the vulgarity of the action, I'm not sure.

Ogden even looked up from his phone for a second.

"I need one per cent on that please," said the man.

"Make sure my wife doesn't come in," said Mountbank once

he had recovered himself. "Perhaps you could put that away."

"I thought you'd want to see it. Like a doctor."

"No. Not in this case."

The man flopped his penis away.

"I'm not sure you really need my help," said Mountbank. "It's big enough."

"You can never have too much of a good thing," said the man. "I'll take whatever percentage I can get on that bad boy."

After the man had paid £1,000 and had his treatment, Mountbank actually laughed. Really laughed.

The man had left, rubbing his newly elongated member through his shorts. "It certainly feels bigger," he said. "Ta."

As the door closed, Mountbank erupted. I'd never seen that before. I'd seen him smile occasionally; a half smile out of the side of his mouth that spoke of mild amusement. Or a closed-lip thin smile which he used for his patients. But never a laugh.

"Did you see that...?" he said as he giggled and shook his head. "Goodness." His whole body shook. "Goodness me... I shan't sleep tonight..."

I found myself laughing too – it was massive after all – but I did note one thing down... Mountbank didn't touch the penis, nor even an approximation of it. Much like the tennis court.

Postscript – a week or so after his consultation I was able to contact the man and ask about his penis, which is a strange conversation to have, although the man was only too delighted to talk about it. It seemed to be his pride and joy and he happily told me about his ambition to be a porn star once, and I quote, "this little fella has had enough stage time on the amateur scene." But I wanted to know if it had actually grown, given that Ogden had declined the opportunity to take before and after measurements. The man replied, "well, I haven't had any complaints so far."

## Chapter 4

# You have found it unwise to be too frank in revealing yourself to others

Ogden, Harry Ogden, Mountbank's Commercial Manager, did his very best not to leave me alone with Mountbank... ever. Ogden wanted to be present when any questions were asked or answered. He wanted to see what I had written in my notes. He wanted to approve any photographs I took. I could never work out exactly why he was so bothered – was he worried that Mountbank, or he himself, would be cast in a negative light to the general public? If so, that ship had long since sailed. Or was it just because he got a thrill from being in control? Given Ogden's illustrious history, I tend towards the latter.

But it was part of the deal – no unsupervised questions. All questions to be submitted in advance. All questions to be confined to specific pre-arranged sessions. General chit-chat was to be avoided and restricted only to platitudes. Ogden didn't say the word platitudes because he'd been a bottom-set kind of kid at school.

"If you speak to him when I'm not there, keep it to the weather and shit yeah?"

Ogden has always been very protective of Mountbank, viewing him, perhaps, as his own private property. Or, at least, as a valuable asset – like a priceless vase perhaps, not to be touched by grubby, enquiring fingers. I said that to Ogden once... about the vase, and he replied:

"More like a prize heifer... you don't want any old bull shafting it..."

Mountbank has never given an interview, except to the police of course. He doesn't have a press officer. He's not on social media. He doesn't have a newsletter or a mailing list. He doesn't do personal appearances. He doesn't endorse anything. He has no sponsorship contracts. He doesn't go to parties, or fundraisers. He won't open your village fete or cut a ribbon on a plaque. He doesn't seem to do anything.

No one really knows that much about him, not in the guise of Archibald Mountbank anyway. Ogden has always been keen to keep it that way. Ogden told me that he regularly turned down significant sums on offer from newspapers and magazines, self-help groups and religious organisations. There was an after-dinner speaking circuit that would pay handsomely for him, but the offers were refused.

"Why?" I asked.

"Air of mystery," he said, as if that explained everything.

Ogden was also careful to keep his own profile relatively low; not including the expensive suits, the sovereign ring and the flash car. Given his chequered past, that is understandable. He seemed to be content; quietly milking Mountbank and taking (I'm guessing) a significant proportion of Mountbank's earnings. Until Mountbank told him that he was planning to retire, and Ogden decided to squeeze as much cash out of this particular cow as possible, before it was too late.

To get to Archibald Mountbank you have to go through Harry Ogden. And how do you get to Harry Ogden when his mobile phone number is regularly changed? Well, quite easily as it happens – particularly if you went to school with him. And particularly if he slept with your wife. Ex-wife.

"Ogden."

That's how he answers the phone. One word. Like some monosyllabic Neanderthal. Or a dickhead, whichever description you prefer.

"Hi Harry, you might not remember me but we went to school together... Ali, Alistair Dodd. We played football together for a bit..."

There was a silence. I wondered if my over-friendly, pally

sort of chat had been too obviously needy.

"Harry?" I said.

"Yeah, I remember you, what do you want? How did you get this number?"

"Julie gave it to me. Julie Blanchard, you remember her? I don't know how she had it."

Silence again. I could almost feel his suspicion through the phone. I didn't exactly expect a warm welcome from him but I didn't expect downright hostility either. It wasn't my fault that he slept with my wife. Ex-wife.

"If you want me to bump you up the line, I can't do it. You'll have to take a ticket like everyone else."

"No, I don't want a ticket. But I did want to speak to you about Mountbank."

"That's the only thing people ever want to speak to me about."

Poor lamb.

"So get to the point. I'm busy."

Twat.

People tend to assume that I dislike Ogden because he had slept with my wife. Ex-wife. Or because he faked cancer for a number of years and pocketed charitable donations. But neither is true, I disliked him before that. I hated him at school. I hated the sneer on his face if you happened to have cheaper trainers than him, which I did. I hated the way he would whine to the referee if anyone bumped into him during football and then whine again when the referee showed him a card for kicking out at an opposing player. I hated it when he put his feet up on a spare seat on the school bus when it was packed full and I hated the fact that no one had the guts to tell him to move his stupid feet so they could sit down. I hated the way in which he made you feel boring – just because you didn't like the things that he liked. I hated the way he'd call you a spastic for reading a book. I hated the way that girls would chase him – even though they knew he was a complete and utter turd.

So, when he faked cancer to elicit sympathy and donations from kind-hearted people, and then obtained a sympathy shag from my wife, ex-wife, it only confirmed my dislike.

How he avoided prison I do not know...

"You might remember that I'm a journalist and..."

"Who with?" he interrupted.

"Freelance."

"Does that mean unemployed?"

"No, it means freelance."

I could feel the sneer on his face.

"So what?"

He sounded like he was doing something else on the other end of the phone. Tapping a keyboard or something.

"I've got a proposition for you."

"You want to see Mountbank? You and everyone else. Right, tell me how much. And don't dick about."

I repeat. Twat.

"Six figures. Just," I said. In truth, at the time of the call, I didn't even have authorisation for the six figures.

There was a silence. I was on the verge of launching into my pre-rehearsed spiel about how I thought it was important to reveal the *Real Mountbank* to the general public as he neared retirement, to get his side of the story before he faded from public view, to slay some myths that might otherwise hound him unto death... all that. But I didn't need it.

"Okay. Just make sure it's well into the six figures. Come to the office on Monday morning. Tell Adam I sent you."

He hung up.

On that first morning Ogden had insisted I pay a non-refundable deposit of £30,000 before he would even discuss arrangements. My editor very nearly didn't pay up. She remembered Ogden from the national press. "Man who faked cancer ordered to repay £28,000 to innocent donors." He made page nine of the Sun, page twenty of the Mirror and even got a little mention in the Guardian. And, as far as I know, he never actually repaid it. Claimed bankruptcy probably.

"Right then, here are the rules," said Ogden once he had checked his account for the cash. "You can sit in on his consultations but you don't interrupt. You don't speak to him unless I'm in the room. You don't speak to his patients without my permission. If you do, this whole thing is off. And I want approval on what you write. Understood?"

I bit my tongue.

"If you're not interested, I'll find someone who is. I could have anyone in that room and they'd pay more than you're paying... so don't dick about."

"So, why'd you pick me?" I asked.

"Because I can control you."

On my fourth day with Mountbank, I was already sick of Ogden and his bloody rules. If I so much as coughed Ogden would give me a warning look. If I did try to talk about the weather or the traffic that morning, Ogden would interrupt, tell me to be quiet. But he did have to leave us alone occasionally, as he did on that fourth afternoon when he left the room to take a call. There was a gap before the next patient – the previous one having stormed out after being quoted £1,000 to increase her vocal range. Why she wanted it, no one was quite sure.

There wasn't enough time for a substitute from the car park. The previous patient had tried to argue and wasn't easy to shift.

Mountbank had his eyes closed.

"Do you think you'll go back to your real name when you retire?" I asked.

Mountbank opened his eyes and stared at me until Ogden returned.

I expected to be shown the door after that – it was in breach of the agreement after all – but no one ever said anything about it.

Postscript – The lady who wanted the increased vocal range returned a few days later, when her rage had died down. She tried to negotiate herself back into the room, saying she was now happy to pay and was sorry for those things she had said in the heat of the moment. But Mrs Mountbank was implacable. She'd had her chance. If she wanted to see Mountbank again, she'd have to take another ticket and wait her turn. The lady threatened to call the police, to call the newspapers, to badmouth Mountbank far and wide... anything she could think of. But Mrs Mountbank just smiled the little half smile that she shared with her husband and waited for the storm to die down. The lady took another ticket.

## Chapter 5

# You pride yourself as an independent thinker and do not accept others' statements without satisfactory proof

"Hi, it's Amy," said a voice down the telephone.

"Amy who?" I asked.

"Amy... remember... we were in Greece together."

Oh, *that Amy*. Tall, blonde-haired Amy. Hard drinking, chain smoking, foul mouthed Amy. We had propped up a number of bars together, whilst pretending to study the confluence between English and Greek literature – or whatever it was we were supposed to be doing. I hadn't seen her since but I wasn't overly surprised to hear from her now. I'd had a number of calls like that in the last week or so. Word had somehow got around that I had access to Mountbank – and the calls from the *Remember Mes* and the *We Have a Mutual Friend* had started to come. People I hadn't seen for years called me up like I was their oldest and dearest friend. My Uncle's friend's god-daughter called me for goodness' sake, hoping for a consultation about her teeth. I started to understand what it might be like for Ogden. No wonder he changed his phone number every couple of months.

"I was wondering if you could get me in to see Mountbank," said Amy. "I need to stop smoking, you see. I thought he could bump up my willpower."

I gave the usual response. No chance. Hell freezing. Not a cat. Snowballs in hot places, etc.

"Oh well, nevermind. I probably wouldn't stop anyway. A four hundred per cent increase might just about do it, but maybe not if I've had a gin and tonic. Anyway, what's he like? That's why I really called."

"Who? Mountbank?"

"Obviously!"

That's what she used to say in Greece if I asked her if she wanted another drink: "obviously."

"I mean, I know he's a conman and probably a pervert," she said, "but what's he like as a person? They say even Hitler loved his dog."

That threw me a bit, as I was just about to say that he was a conman and a pervert. Virtually everyone I had spoken to in the last couple of weeks had wanted to talk about Mountbank, but most were satisfied when they received confirmation that he was indeed a conman and a pervert – just like they'd read in the papers or seen on the TV.

Only my mum disagreed.

"Think you know everything don't you? You young people. Believe me... if you'd seen what I'd seen you might not be so definite."

I hadn't seen what she'd seen, but I'd certainly heard about it often enough. My mum would tell anyone and everyone, regardless of whether they'd heard the story before, about how a spirit had deadheaded all the red flowers in her shop one Tuesday night in 1989. She had been a florist and had prepared a fine display for a funeral when the mysterious moment occurred. Opened her eyes to the spirit world, she always said.

"There's more to this world than can be measured with a ruler," she said to me over Sunday lunch. I bit my tongue, as I always did when she told that stupid story.

What was Mountbank like, as a person? How do you answer that?

What was Hitler like, as a person? Did he really love his dog? Was that an urban myth? What about Mussolini? Or Saddam Hussein? Or Jack the Ripper? Would they make good dinner-party guests? Would you ever say, "Oh, he's alright as long as you don't get him going on the Jewish question?"

"He's...," I couldn't quite find the right word. How do you

describe such a man as Mountbank? "Nice."

Amy laughed. She had a cackle that brought back memories of vast quantities of Ouzo and nightclubs that didn't even open until 2am.

"Nice? Archibald Mountbank is nice?"

I think I was as surprised as she was, when that word came out of my mouth.

"Erm, yes."

"I thought you'd hate him?"

"I do."

"But you still think he's nice?"

"Maybe I should have said 'polite' or 'courteous' or something like that. Pleasant."

"Well, I never... nice... that is not a word I thought I'd ever hear you say. Pleasant! Had a personality transplant or something?"

I suppose I may have been quite outspoken during my time in Greece, in my pretentious student days. I was a fan of denouncing things – like the freeloading Royal Family or corrupt Tory politicians. I had a lot to say about the Greek economy. I wrote a searing article on the banking crisis for my university newspaper that wasn't published. I signed a lot of petitions. Free Palestine. Save the Whales. Something to do with the Gurkhas. And I just loved, really loved, staying up late into the night and debunking conspiracy theories. If someone said to me that they believed the Americans were behind the attack on the Twin Towers, I was off. Amy had sat through no end of those diatribes, waiting for another drink.

Mountbank should have been right up my street. He was up my street. It's hard to think of a more universally and vocally disliked man. He is, without a doubt, one of the biggest conmen in history. And a pervert, albeit a rather restrained one. And yet he is... nice.

"Do you actually like him?"

I hesitated...

"A bit," I admitted.

If you forget the charlatanism for a moment... there's a lot to like about him. He gives every impression of being a devoted husband. Mrs Mountbank is his childhood sweetheart; they'd been together for over fifty years. Ogden tells me that Mountbank gives huge swathes of money to charity, anonymously of course. I've never heard him be rude, or unkind. Until recently, he lived in the same terraced house that he had lived in his entire adult life. He only moved because he had to. He wears V-neck jumpers and tartan socks. He doesn't have a Rolex, or a Lamborghini. I'm not even sure if he owns a mobile phone. If he does, I've never seen it. And to my knowledge there has never been a kiss-and-tell story about him, no call girl describing her night of passion with mystical Mountbank! Nor has there ever been any lurid revelations about his private life. No orgies, sado-masochism or rent boys tied up in his basement. He's squeaky clean, except for the police interviews of course. And even that came to nothing, in the end.

You could even convince yourself that he was just being kind and gentlemanly when he laid his hairy hands on the young girls who walked through his door. And the fact that he didn't lay his hands on many of the men – the huge penis-man being a prime example... was just a coincidence.

It's like what I always used to say about the Queen: "I do hate her, but only as an institution. As a little old lady, she's quite nice."

"You're not falling for him, are you?" Amy asked, with a laugh.

"No. Of course not."

There had been a moment, a few days before the phone call, that had caused me to reassess my view of Mountbank. Just a little. A young lad had entered the consulting room, visibly terrified. He was shaking and could barely get his words out.

He was a young Muslim lad and, as he eventually revealed, gay.

"Those things don't mix Mr Mountbank. My parents…"

He couldn't finish that sentence.

"Can you please make me one per cent less… homosexual… please? Or one per cent more heterosexual, please? Just anything, please."

Mountbank stared at the young lad, one of his tricks, until we were all starting to feel a little uncomfortable.

"I can't help you," he said eventually.

"Please Mr Mountbank…"

I readied my pen. Would this be the moment when I could pin something on him? None of this abstract, placebo, widow's mite crap… none of this faith-healing, consensual touching, surveying the soil bullshit… something definite. Some actual prejudice. Some Islamophobic homophobia on which I could hang my book.

"I can't help you," said Mountbank in his soft voice, "because there is nothing wrong with you. You're fine as you are. You should never try to change who you are. Fundamentally, we are who we are."

Bloody hell, I hadn't expected that.

"But my parents…"

"It is your parents who need help. Send them to me and I will increase their empathy, their tolerance."

The young lad left the office in a strange state of disappointment and affirmation. Ogden shook his head as no fee (donation) was charged. I was shaking mine as a sensational scoop had just melted away in front of me. Mountbank just closed his eyes, waiting for his next appointment.

"You're not falling for him, are you?" asked Amy.

"No. Of course not."

"Lots of people have," Amy warned.

"Not me."

Postscript – The young lad came out to his parents a week or two after his encounter with Mountbank. I'm afraid to say that it didn't go well. When I caught up with him, he had moved out of the family home. He seemed okay though... not happy, but relieved somehow.

## Chapter 6

# At times you have serious doubts as to whether you have made the right decision or done the right thing

Appearances can be deceptive, I suppose, but it always seemed to me that Mr and Mrs Mountbank were very much in love. Childhood sweethearts, as I've said. They were as close to inseparable as a couple could be. They spent more time together in a single day than I did with my wife (ex-wife) in my entire marriage. But then again, she was busy shagging Ogden.

They would arrive at the office together, the Mountbanks, often holding hands. She would bring him tea or coffee at regular intervals throughout the day. He'd touch her hand or say thank you each time. They would make eye contact and share a smile, that closed-lip smile of theirs. They would lunch together in the consulting room, talking quietly and eating sandwiches that Mrs Mountbank must have prepared that morning.

It was comical.

When I first saw Mountbank drinking from a small carton of juice that he had taken from his lunchbox, I almost laughed. He looked like a child, sucking on a little straw from a cheap carton of juice. His blue plastic lunchbox was perched on his knees, always on the verge of tipping off.

Mrs Mountbank looked almost as ridiculous, sitting opposite him in the chair usually reserved for clients, with her lunchbox identically perched. She always dressed so formally, or should I say traditionally; long skirts and brooches; a nice cardigan and the occasional scarf. To see her eating a packet of crisps with her delicate fingers – beef and onion – was almost ridiculous. It was a multipack too, not to be sold separately.

It always confused me... that these multi-millionaires should be making their own packed lunches.

They could have had their own chef on hand to attend to their every culinary whim. They could have ordered in. They could have booked out an entire restaurant to ensure they weren't disturbed. But no, they had a thin sandwich each, on white bread, followed by a packet of crisps and a tangerine. Nothing more beyond the morning and afternoon biscuits that Mrs Mountbank served with the tea. I soon found out that these biscuits were as plain as the Mountbanks themselves. Ogden, as you would expect, refused his offer of a biscuit – preferring to slip outside for a quick smoke or to make a call whilst Mrs Mountbank was shielding her husband from my unauthorised questions.

It irritated me... I mean, what's the point of being one of the richest people in Britain if you're just going to buy small cartons of economy orange juice? I bloody wouldn't.

At the end of the working day, they would slide together into the backseat of their car and Adam, their bodyguard/chauffeur/doorman, would drive them home.

"What do they do in the evenings?" I asked Ogden.

He didn't answer. Just gave me one of his looks.

I suppose they could have been up to anything within the private confines of their large country mansion, protected by CCTV and hefty security gates. They could have been up all night engaging in wild sexual orgies, sacrificing goats and worshipping the devil. They could have been leading a life of complete and utter debauchery; sex, drugs and rock and roll – burning money just for the sheer hell of it, snorting cocaine from the firm bodies of modern-day minimum wage slaves and laughing darkly as they celebrated yet another day of embezzling cash from various gullible innocents.

But it seemed more likely that they did a crossword together or perhaps listened to a gramophone record with their eyes closed.

I wondered if they even had any friends. Even Charles Ponzi, the greatest swindler of recent times, had friends. Who would he have sold his coupons to in the first place otherwise? Conmen were supposed to be gregarious, sociable types, with a fluid self-confidence that made them at home in any setting. But I never heard either of the Mountbanks refer to anything that might suggest a social life.

So, there you go... nice. Inoffensive. Polite. Humble even.

This greedy, money-grabbing, predatory, cheating, exploitative, heartless shyster wasn't living up to expectations. My editor, as you might imagine, was furious.

My book was shaping up to be phenomenally dull.

I tried asking Mountbank what he did of an evening, again, when Ogden had left the room, but he just stared at me in the same way that he had when I asked him about his name. Those were the first and the third questions I'd asked. The second had gone down just as well.

"Is there anyone you wouldn't charge for your services?"

I hadn't meant it as a criticism or a rebuke, it was a genuine question. He charged (sorry, I mean he kindly suggested that a voluntary donation might be appreciated) everyone who came through the door, regardless of their predicament. The more vain or greedy the motivation, the higher the price. The more desperate and painful, the lower the price. But everyone paid, without exception. Those who were ill, or those suffering through no fault of their own, only had to pay a nominal fee of ten pounds – towards utilities, Mountbank said. Ogden would always roll his eyes when Mountbank quoted such a low figure and he accepted the money in obvious bad grace. Anyone who couldn't pay would be removed from the office immediately, denied the life-changing benefits of Mountbank's magic hands. Even if they were wheeled out on a trolley.

The voluntary donation didn't seem that voluntary if you got kicked out of the room for non-payment.

I was trying to ask whether there was anything so close to his heart that he would expend his powers for free. He didn't respond.

Cancer patients... ten pounds.

Multiple sclerosis... ten pounds.

Bipolar... ten pounds.

Would he waive his fee for a child with brain disease? Or a professor with dementia? A childless couple? What? He wouldn't say. He just closed his eyes again.

My editor wasn't impressed.

"All you're doing is describing Mountbank's day. I didn't pay six figures for a surveillance report!"

I tried Mrs Mountbank.

Mrs Mountbank can only be described as a cold fish. She is a reserved woman – slightly taller than her husband but equally thin and serious and quiet. Her hair is neat and grey. Her clothes are functional, traditional – but stopping well short of elegance. I suspect that both Mr and Mrs Mountbank buy their clothes from the same shop – one dealing in muted autumnal colours at reasonable prices. She smiles as rarely as her husband but she is always polite. She deals with the various supplicants, who range from the tearful to the angry, from the anxious to the embarrassed, calmly and gently.

"I'm afraid he won't see you unless you have a ticket."

"No, I'm afraid I can't give you any preferential treatment."

"I'm sorry but only one person is allowed in the waiting room at a time."

She was so polite and so reserved that I could never work out whether she liked me or not. She was certainly suspicious of me, that much I know. She would often cast a glance at my notepad as she brought tea for her husband – no doubt wondering what was in it. Very little of any interest as it happens. And she seemed to see a potential barb in every question I asked.

"I was just wondering where the best place is to get a

sandwich," I asked her. I didn't need or want to know, but I was just curious to see if I could get a conversation going with her. I needed something.

"I'm afraid I wouldn't know," she said.

"I suppose you don't get into town much?" I asked.

"No."

"Do you ever wish you could? Have a little stroll around town? Buy some bits and bobs. Pop to the bank. I suppose you get bothered an awful lot."

"Not really."

"Must be an odd existence..."

"I'm very sorry, Mr Dodd, but I'm afraid I have a number of things to do. If you'll excuse me..."

I don't think it had helped that I had been introduced as Ogden's friend. As reserved as Mrs Mountbank was, it wasn't hard to detect her distaste for Ogden. And I couldn't blame her for that.

"Archie, this is my friend – Alistair Dodd. I told him he could sit in and watch."

Even I had flinched when Ogden had described me as his friend. Twat.

I expected the notoriously private Archibald Mountbank to be a little curious or suspicious about me on that first morning, but he just said, "Fine," and gave me a tight little smile of welcome before closing his eyes again.

Mrs Mountbank – dressed in flowery patterns – was less relaxed.

"Why?" she asked of Ogden.

"Why what?"

"Why is he sitting in?"

"Because I said so," Ogden said, as he smiled sweetly at Mrs Mountbank. She smiled back; a closed-lip smile that I would see on her husband's face quite soon.

"Get him a coffee, will you?"

"Of course," she said. "How do you have it?" she asked me.

"He'll get what he's given," Ogden said before I could answer.

Mrs Mountbank – ever the polite example of gracious womanhood, complied.

But one thing I did note, the only blot I could ever detect in the picture of marital bliss – Mrs Mountbank never, ever, sat in on a consultation. She never saw where Mountbank put his hands.

# Chapter 7

# 'You prefer a certain amount of change and variety and become dissatisfied when hemmed in by restrictions and limitations

"Don't complain – I did exactly what you wanted."

I was in a position that I never thought I would be in – sitting in a pub with Harry Ogden, having a pint of beer and trying to call upon his good graces. I'd been in plenty of pubs with him before, but we were mainly on other sides of the bar mingling with different groups of friends. Well, I had friends. He had a series of attractive conquests and a few idiots who hung on his every word. And, as far as I know, he has no good graces.

"Come on Harry, I need more. My editor is losing it," I said.

"Not my fault. You're the journalist."

"Well I can't do a lot if you won't let me speak to him."

"You have been speaking to him though, haven't you, sunshine?"

He gave me one of his most sneering grins.

"Yes," I admitted.

"Yeah, Mountbank told me. You asked him about his real name. Shouldn't have done that, sunshine. He's touchy."

"What am I supposed to ask him about? If he's not touchy about something then you are."

"He's my retirement fund... got to look after him."

I took a large pull at my drink. It was either that or throw it all over Ogden's head. I needed to change tack.

"How did you get involved with him anyway?" I asked, after a while.

I hadn't kept in contact with Ogden after school, for obvious reasons. I'd gone off to university. He'd embarked on a number of entrepreneurial endeavours... all of which, I am pleased to say, failed dramatically. He ran a karaoke bar which closed after a few months. He bought and sold luxury cars, but bought more than he sold. He even ran a pet shop. Then came his period of disgrace. Relative disgrace.

"You wouldn't believe me," he said.

"Try me."

Ogden fiddled with his nose and gave me a long, hard stare. For a minute I thought he was going to tell me to take a running jump. But eventually he said:

"He healed my cancer."

"You never had cancer."

"Didn't I?"

"No."

"I've got a doctor's report that said I did."

"You've also got a suspended sentence that says you didn't."

Ogden laughed. He liked being goaded. I smiled, because I liked goading him.

"Believe what you want, but, I tell you, I was dying until he laid his hands on me."

Ogden met my gaze and held my stare. He didn't flinch, he didn't fiddle – none of the usual traits associated with lying. It seemed... genuine. I did wonder where Mountbank had placed his hands, but thought I'd hold on to that question.

"And one per cent saved your life did it?"

Ogden had claimed to have thyroid cancer. Found a swelling on his neck, constant sore throat, hoarse voice. You can imagine what the papers made of that. Ogden's sad little face on page twenty-seven of a national newspaper... *I just thought I was losing my voice until I discovered...* It made a wonderful alarmist piece. Ogden became quite the local celebrity. *Tragic story of young businessman...who once had trials to become a professional footballer.* The prognosis was not good.

Ogden, despite the terrible news, bravely volunteered to raise funds for a cancer research charity. He did a sponsored walk, and accepted donations from a varied assortment of well-wishers. He didn't want it for himself, of course. It was too late for him. He was just holding the money until he could make a sizeable donation to one of the established charities, or perhaps he'd use the money to send an orphan to Disney World. There was even talk of a Harry Ogden Foundation. And then, suddenly, he was in remission and the money had gone.

I covered the trial and I bloody loved it.

"Who said anything about one per cent?" Ogden said with a smug smile.

"What?"

"You heard."

Now here was something that my editor might actually be interested in.

"He can do more than one per cent at a time?" I asked.

It sounded odd. Mountbank's entire ethos was built around the one per cent. He was the Marginal Man. The Minimalist Miracle Worker. The King of Fine Degrees. His unique selling point was built upon the barely perceptible, the hard to measure. It's what kept him in business.

And if he was for real... actually for real... if he could bestow more than one per cent at a time... why didn't he? Think of the lives he could have saved.

I kicked myself for even thinking that stupid thought. *Think of the lives he could have saved.* What an idiot. He couldn't have saved any lives, because he's a conman – a millionaire conman who trades on the hopes and dreams of gullible idiots. Why did I need to remind myself of that? I was getting sucked in... just by the sheer ordinariness of the man and his cardboard cut-out wife. It's hard to sustain hate and distrust towards a man whose greatest pleasure in life appears to be a Bourbon biscuit at 10.30 every morning.

"He can do more than one per cent at a time?"

"He can do whatever he wants, he's Archibald Mountbank."

If this were true...

I kicked myself again... after all, I was speaking to Harry Ogden, a serial liar, adulterer and an all-round precious example of what it is to be a twat. Of course he hadn't given Ogden more than one per cent. He hadn't given him anything.

The whole point was not to give more than one per cent.

"Anyway, I've got you a present," said Ogden as he got a piece of paper out of his pocket. "Here's a list of a few people you should probably speak to. Clients. Now don't say I don't ever do anything for you."

He handed over a small piece of paper but snatched it back before I could actually take it.

"Now this makes us even doesn't it... for shagging your wife?"

Ex-wife.

## Chapter 8

# Some of your aspirations tend to be pretty unrealistic

The list that Ogden gave me was virtually useless.

He probably knew that when he gave it to me. I probably knew it too but I went through the list anyway. My editor was getting tetchy, to the extent that I'd stopped answering her calls where possible. I rang through the list:

"Good morning, my name is Alistair Dodd, I'm a journalist and I'm currently working on a book about Archibald Mountbank and I understand you…"

Beep.

The first seven people on the list just hung up on me… some being ruder than others in the process. Quite a few said, "how did you get this number?" before disconnecting. A couple of them sounded rattled before claiming I'd been misinformed.

The list did add a bit of substance to some of the existing rumours, but it didn't actually prove anything. At this rate, my book was going to be no more than a rehash of what had already appeared in various tabloid newspapers and other tittle-tattle periodicals. I almost tore the list up at one point but refrained when I realised that I could put a photostat of the list into my book. It wasn't that I thought Ogden's handwritten note would particularly convince anyone, but it would at least fill a page.

Occasionally I would have to check in with my editor. She was starting to get angry… suggesting that I might like to ask Ogden for the money back. That would have gone down like a lead balloon. So I kept trying with the list.

One of the country's most high profile sporting teams gave me a terse "no comment" phone interview that lasted about one minute. I had asked whether there was any truth to the rumour that the team had used Mountbank, but they stone-walled me. That was closely followed by a letter from their solicitor which stated that any further dissemination of the rumours would result in the full force of the law being brought upon me. My publisher's lawyer disagreed, as the rumour was already in the public domain. So that rumour, for the sake of completeness, was that Mountbank had increased the amount of red blood cells in each of the team's contracted athletes – to give them the slight edge needed in endurance events. Hard one to prove... as that particular sports organisation was winning everything before they supposedly met with Mountbank, and they won everything after... so who could tell? But I could certainly imagine the soft-voiced charlatan placing his hands on each of the athlete's thighs, whilst spouting some of his semi-spiritual mumbo jumbo.

"Endurance of the mind goes further than endurance of the body."

One of the world's most prominent opera singers ignored my email.

A former page three model told me to "sod off."

The British Army threatened to have me shot, but I think that may have been a joke on the part of an overly gregarious media liaison officer. He had even used a German accent.

"Come on...," I said, "it's superhero stuff isn't it... genetically modified soldiers... one per cent stronger and fitter and more deadly... one per cent better at shooting and bombing and killing... one per cent better at protecting their country... surely you want to talk to me about that... even if only to tell me how ridiculous it all is?"

"Ve vill have you shot!"

An actor, somewhat of a national treasure but struggling to remember his lines as he got older, did give me a quote on the understanding that he would not be named. He had accepted a large sum of money to appear in a West End revival of a Terrance

Rattigan play... but was in danger of being re-cast, despite being a knight of the realm and a generally good egg.

"I don't know if he improved my memory or not, but he made me feel as if he did, so that was worth the £100,000 I paid him."

"But surely you weren't getting paid that much for the play?" I asked.

"It's legacy dear boy, it's legacy. You can't put a price on that."

No one wanted to admit to having seen Archibald Mountbank, Improver Extraordinaire. It was frustrating. I could understand if the visit had been for some embarrassing or furtive reason... vanity or greed... but just warding off the ravages of time or a deadly illness, I didn't see what was shameful in that. Stupid maybe, but not shameful. But still, no one wanted to confess.

There was a time when Mountbank had been all the rage. He was quite the celebrity sweetheart at one point. The general public were fascinated, rather than repulsed, by him. He was a conversation starter. People wondered if he could be the real deal. Students wrote papers about him. Psychologists analysed his methods. Celebrities flocked to him. Having secured an audience with him was a mark of distinction and an absolute must-mention at a dinner party. A few copycats sprung up around the country, offering immediate consultations for those who didn't want to join the end of the Mountbank queue, but most people wanted the Real McCoy and would gladly wait. For about two years, Mountbank was in fashion.

That was until Ada Banks went to see Mountbank for a consultation.

Ada Banks was an extremely photogenic woman in her late thirties, with a tall, dark handsome husband, two adorable children and less than six months to live. She had reached a dead end with the NHS and certain private hospitals. So, she went to see Mountbank.

He gave her one per cent of something to help with her terminal illness. She lived long enough to stop taking her medication and rewrite her will, bequeathing a huge sum to Mountbank. The subsequent lawsuit, criminal investigation and media outcry very quickly made Mountbank unfashionable. A photo of Ada Banks, smiling over her shoulder, was everywhere. It featured in every Mountbank-related story for years, often next to a hazy photo of Mountbank looking furtive. The implication was clear... look at this beautiful woman and the man who abused her trust.

After that, the great and good of this nation were queueing up to publicly denounce Mountbank, even if they continued to queue up for his treatments privately. Having secured an audience with Mountbank suddenly became something clandestine.

But fortunately, one man did agree to talk to me.

Adam Durlitz.

Adam Durlitz was, if you remember, a British sprinter who received a lifetime ban from the sport for a number of doping violations. He'd never been in the top tier of world sprinters, but he'd made a decent living and won a few titles and snaffled a few promotional opportunities. He advertised cheese and crackers, for some bizarre reason. He'd first tested positive after winning a silver medal in a World Championship relay event and had quickly become a figure of hate across the country.

"Disgrace. Cheat. Greed."

One thing this country can't abide is cheating at sport... unless it's football.

He was happy to speak to me on the basis that I gave him some money and bought him breakfast.

I interviewed him in a greasy spoon cafe in Leicester called Ted's where a mug of tea was only 59 pence. Madness.

"He laid his hands on my thighs, right on my thighs let me tell you, and increased the number of fast-twitch muscle fibres by one per cent," said Adam as he tucked into a full English breakfast. By the look of him, it wasn't the only full English breakfast he had been tucking into recently.

He was spooning the food in at some pace, as if he were afraid someone would take it away from him in the same way that they had removed his World Championship medal.

"And I tell you, if you want proof, I'll tell you this, before I saw him, I could run a hundred metres in ten seconds flat. My first race after... 9.98."

"You don't think it was a placebo?"

"A what?" he asked, mouth full of egg.

"Like something that... erm... doesn't matter. Could it have been coincidence?"

"Doubt it mate, I tell you, I'd been running ten seconds flat for about eleven months before that. Just couldn't break it. Not even in training. Let me tell you, I'd reached my limit. I weren't gonna get any quicker than that, not without help."

Adam seemed convinced. And hungry.

"What about the drugs?" I asked.

I was a bit worried about bringing it up. No one likes to be confronted with their own stupidity or their own dishonesty. But Adam wasn't bothered. He just carried on chewing and talking.

"That was after. He wouldn't see me again, Mountbank. Said I had to get another ticket, go to the back of the queue. And let me tell you, I couldn't wait that long, could I? There was an Olympics coming up and I weren't going to get anywhere with 9.98, let me tell you. That's when I took the drugs. The first time anyway."

The findings of the doping enquiry did dispute that, but I thought I better not bring it up. The toxicology report suggested that Adam had been doping from the very beginning of his career. He denied it and continues to deny and, given his reputation and his waistline, I'm not sure why he would continue to lie.

"I said to Mountbank, if he just worked with me for a week, I could have been the best in the world, broke some records. But he wasn't interested, said he had other people to see. Said something about a seed growing through the soil or something, but I didn't know what he was going on about."

I had heard Mountbank use that line and I wasn't sure what it meant either.

"I offered some money to that guy... who's that flash dickhead who looks after Mountbank?"

"Harry Ogden?"

"That's him... I tell you I offered him all sorts... but that did no good either. I would have given sexual favours if it had got me in to see Mountbank again, but no dice. So, I took the drugs."

He stuffed a hash brown into his mouth.

"Do you regret it?" I asked.

There was no hesitation. "The drugs yes. Seeing Mountbank, no. It's not cheating with him, is it? It's all natural. He's a genius, let me tell you. A miracle worker. And you can quote me on that."

"So, you'd use him again?"

"Absolutely. Wouldn't you? You've seen him working. You must know what he can do."

I took a sip of my 59 pence mug of tea and tried to be a coolly detached journalist... rather than just laugh spitefully in his gullible, deluded face.

"I can't say I'm entirely convinced."

"Ah well, the thing with Mountbank is...," said Adam as he took a bite of some fried bread and then pointed his fork at me, "you won't believe in him until you need him."

## Chapter 9

# You have a great need for other people to like and admire you

The offer came completely out of the blue. Mountbank had just finished with a violinist who wanted to be one per cent more proficient in the higher registers. Not because he wanted to become some sort of international superstar, but because he wanted to keep his job. He played with some orchestra or other and those not hitting the required standard were dealt with ruthlessly. It was those people that I felt most sorry for – the ones clinging to the bottom rung of the ladder. For every athlete who wanted his marginal gains to chase a world record, there were ten semi-professionals who just wanted to keep providing for their families. For every model wanting to be one per cent better looking to secure another lucrative contract, there were ten middle aged men who wanted to be one per cent better looking because they were worried that their wives might leave them.

So many people came to see Mountbank just because they were desperate to cling on to something. Wives, looks, dreams, memories. Desperate people take desperate measures. I felt bad for them.

And I also felt sorry for them because they were being fleeced. Their desperation was preyed upon – even if Mountbank wasn't necessarily your run-of-the-mill predator, what with his sleepy eyes and his hairy hands and his comfortable knitwear and his one-dimensional wife.

The violinist had left with the assurance that his musical ability had been increased, and with £100 less in his pocket. Ogden had rolled his eyes, as he did every time anything less than five figures was charged. I was just writing down some more profound bullshit that Mountbank had dredged up from somewhere:

"When a musician plays, it isn't what he plays that is important, but rather what he *doesn't* play."

I was surprised the violinist didn't hit Mountbank or walk out. I was tempted myself. Utter crap. But the violinist was nodding in agreement. Idiot.

"Mr Dodd," said Mountbank after the violinist had left, "my wife and I were wondering if you might like to have dinner with us?"

It was pretty much the first thing he had said to me, besides an occasional "good morning" or an "excuse me." It was almost certainly the first fully formed sentence he had used on me.

I glanced at Ogden but he just gave me a raised eyebrow look and then went back to his phone. I wasn't sure if that meant he had arranged the thing or that he was pretending to.

So there I was, in my car later that evening, pulling up outside the huge security gates at the Mountbank residence. I couldn't even see the house as I pressed the intercom and waited to be admitted. The place was well screened by a tall wall and even bigger trees. It may have been my imagination, but the trees did look slightly bigger than normal trees. Mountbank had probably increased their capacity to grow.

After a moment or two I was buzzed in. The security gates swung wide and I drove down the gravel driveway, past manicured lawns, sculptures, a sundial and countless rose bushes. And the house, a mile or so down the drive, was large, tall and red. A proper country mansion.

It was the architectural opposite of a V-neck jumper and a flowery blouse.

It didn't seem the kind of place that the Mountbanks would choose, and perhaps it wasn't. They only moved into the mansion a couple of years ago, after various threats on their lives and numerous breakages to their property. There are only so many times that you can receive a death threat through your letterbox, or have your tyres slashed, before you decide to move house. Their previous house had been a modest mid-terrace in the local market town. It had been the first house they had bought when they married and it only had two bedrooms. They still own it... according to the Land Registry. Of course, there is no Mr and Mrs Archibald Mountbank on the title deeds – but rather a Tony and Veronica Griffiths.

Mountbank was waiting on the steps leading to the huge house, hands in pockets, as I drove in.

"Welcome," he said, "just leave your car there – there's no one else coming."

"Not Harry?" I asked.

"No."

"Well, I guess he's here quite a lot," I said, digging.

Mountbank stopped to think.

"Hm, I don't think he's actually ever been here."

I tried to hide my delight.

"Come in," he said.

He led me into the huge house. We stepped into a cavernous hallway, but Mountbank immediately turned left and I followed him into a small sitting room. Mrs Mountbank was waiting, looking as prim and proper as ever. She had a string of pearls around her neck, although it could easily have been a string of white beads. What did they spend their money on? The house was the only ostentatious aspect of their entire lives.

I recited my carefully worded opening line.

"Mrs Mountbank, can I just say that I'm honoured to be invited here. I know you don't have many guests."

"You're very welcome, and please, call me Veronica."

"So, you kept...?"

The words were out before I could stop them. Idiot. I was determined not to be too inquisitive or to pry too much, not before dessert anyway – but it just popped out. I had a definite plan... small talk and compliments before dinner, some general talk about his consultancy business during the main course and then... bam, onto the hard stuff during dessert... like the death threats, and the court cases and the police interviews and the general attitude of shameful exploitation of the masses. But I cocked it up straight away.

"Yes, I kept my former name."

Dozens of follow-up questions popped into my head but I bit down on the words.

"Can I offer you a drink, Mr Dodd?" asked Mrs Mountbank. I struggled to think of her as a Veronica. "We don't have any alcohol I'm afraid."

Typical of these people... the appearance of purity.

"Just water then please," I said. "Oh, and please call me Alistair. Or Ali, if you like."

"Of course, Alistair. Will tap water suffice?"

"Certainly."

Veronica slipped out of the room.

Mountbank was leaning against a wall, eyes closed – again. That was starting to bug me, all the closed eye business. He couldn't be that tired, surely. All he did was sit in a comfortable chair all day long selling false hope. Not too taxing. Maybe Veronica was a sex-obsessed nymphomaniac, who kept him up all night with her sexual shenanigans. Or maybe he sat up all night counting his ill-gotten gains. I was determined to ask him if he was narcoleptic, probably over coffee... if I got that far.

"This place is huge," I said, "how many rooms has it got?"

Mountbank opened his eyes, blinked, thought, and said, "I've no idea," before closing his eyes again.

Veronica came back with a glass of tap water and said, "come on now Tony, eyes open tonight. We have a guest."

Tony...?

"Of course."

Mountbank stood up straight and opened his eyes wider

than normal. He gave me that closed-lip smile.

"I'm afraid we don't have fancy food Mr Dodd... I mean Alistair. Just simple."

"Just my kind of thing..." I lied.

A few minutes later we were sitting around a small circular table in the corner of their kitchen. It was so small. I wondered if it had been designed as some sort of servants' quarters. There must have been a kitchen somewhere in that building bigger than my actual house but, if there was, we weren't in it.

"This is cosy," I said, because we were all uncomfortably close. My wife (ex-wife) always said I had intimacy issues but even she would have admitted that this eating arrangement was slightly too tactile. At the start of the main course, both Mountbank and I reached for the salt at the same time and I got a touch of his hairy hand. It was the first time I'd made any physical contact with him... we hadn't so much as brushed shoulders in my time with him to date. I didn't feel any different afterwards.

Veronica hadn't made a starter, although there was a bowl of salted crisps available for grazing. I imagined that these had been decanted from a multipack of economy crisps, like the ones they had in their matching lunchboxes. The main meal was lasagne with a fresh green salad from a bag, followed by Eton Mess for dessert. It was... nice. Boring. Inexpensive.

Sticking to the plan, I tried a bit of small talk whilst I nibbled a crisp.

"Do you always eat in here?"

"Yes."

"But you've got the biggest house in Britain," I said, exaggerating a bit in an effort to generate some bonhomie.

"Harry thought it would be a good investment," said Mountbank. "I think."

That was the end of that strand of bonhomie. What else could I dredge up?

"You must have a few acres…?"

"I've no idea," said Mountbank. "Do we have a few acres, dear?"

"Yes, I think we must."

I was going to say something about business rates as I started my lasagne when Mrs Mountbank, Veronica, said:

"I suppose you're wondering why we invited you here?"

It did vaguely cross my mind that this is the kind of thing a serial killer might say as a prelude to chopping you into bits. Maybe that was their thing? I wondered vaguely if I should look up whether any of their clients had mysteriously disappeared over the years. Now, that would sell some books. Fraud, conman and murderer.

"Yes," I said.

I thought they had invited me over to lay on the charm, or perhaps to bribe me, or to justify themselves. I had given Ogden an early draft of the first two chapters of my book and they were not complimentary. I didn't doubt that he had told the Mountbanks. I wondered if they had finally woken up to the hatchet job I was planning on them. But it seemed not.

"I'm dying, Mr Dodd," said Mountbank, as if he was just asking me to pass the water jug.

# Chapter 10

# You have a tendency to be critical of yourself

I have ten GCSEs. I have three A-levels. I have a degree. I'm getting close to forty years of age. I don't believe in Father Christmas. I don't believe what I read in the newspapers. I know politicians are careful with the truth. I don't believe that a face cream can reverse the ravages of time. I don't believe you can get a six pack without any effort. I know there's no such thing as a free lunch.

I'm not an idiot. Not in the conventional sense anyway.

I wouldn't describe myself as a cynic as such, but I do have a healthy level of scepticism. I'm a journalist for goodness' sake.

And, so, when Mountbank told me he was dying, I was instantly suspicious. Or disbelieving. It wasn't easy for me to believe anything that came out of his mouth, not when his entire life was built on a lie. If he told me he liked ham sandwiches, I would have probably thought he preferred cheese.

"Is that why you're retiring?" I asked, after Mountbank had revealed the big news.

I was relieved to be getting down to business at last. I suppose I should have opened up with a condolence or a "I'm sorry to hear that."

"Yes."

"What is it? Cancer?"

"No, not cancer."

"Well, what then? Heart disease?"

"No, not that."

Mountbank gave me his close-lipped smile. Say no more.

"Well, whatever it is... can't you just heal yourself?"

Mr and Mrs Mountbank shared a wry smile...

"That is one thing I can't do," said Mountbank.

Veronica leaned over and squeezed her husband's hairy hand.

"I think you might need to explain more, Tony," said Veronica.

"Explain what?" I asked.

Mountbank took a breath:

"Why do you think I only deal in one per cents?" began Mountbank.

Because you're an evidence-shy conman...

"It's because every per cent that I give away depletes me by the corresponding amount."

Veronica squeezed Mountbank's hand, as if he had taken some mightily significant step. As if he'd declared his alcoholism, or admitted some great crime. They stared at me as if something profound had been said. Had it?

"What do you mean?"

"He's killing himself, Mr Dodd," said Veronica, with some force. "He's giving away a piece of his soul every time he treats someone. He's taking one per cent off his life span and giving it to others."

We sat in silence for a moment... as we all took some time to let the bollocks settle into the atmosphere around us. What is the opposite of a truth bomb? One per cent of his soul. Bloody hell – who did they take me for?

"Shouldn't he be dead by now? He must have seen more than 100 people... one per cent at a time... dead."

"Your maths is lacking... as is your empathy," said Mountbank.

Lacking in empathy? I'd been sitting in his bloody consulting room for weeks, listening to him trot out his psychobabble platitudes and watching him fondling every third patient... and not once had I said anything... not once had I begged his gullible patients to save their money... what do you call bloody empathy if not that? Lacking!

But I do accept that my maths was wrong.

"He's seventy-two years old for God's sake... not bad for a man voluntarily ending his own life!"

Neither of the Mountbanks responded to that, which was annoying.

"So, when is he going to die then?"

"We're not sure."

"So how do you know he's dying?"

"I can just feel it," said Mountbank.

"He's wearing out," said Veronica. "Surely you can see it."

And the horrible thing was, the next time I sat in Mounbank's consultation room, with his hands on a young man looking for more movement in his mangled little finger, I thought I saw it... Mountbank diminishing before my eyes.

The slightest degradation in his skin, a hint of an additional line around his mouth, sweat around his sunken eyes.

"Is that why you close your eyes so much?" I asked.

"One of them. I'm tired."

"So, what do you want me to do? Make you into a martyr? Is that why you invited me here?"

"No," said Mountbank, "I just want you to open your eyes. I'm not a fake."

## Chapter 11

# Your sexual adjustment has presented problems for you

I ignored her the first five times, but then I thought I had better answer. I was worried it might be something about the dog. I still love that dog.

"What?" I asked.

I deal with my wife (ex-wife) in the same way that Ogden deals with the entire world – that is, terse, unfriendly and suspicious. And, if possible, with single syllables.

"Hi," she said. "Are you okay?"

"I'm fine. What do you want?"

I had managed to avoid my wife (ex-wife) for nearly two years. She'd rung a few times, particularly in the months immediately after the split, leaving messages such as:

"Can we still be friends?" or

"Could we at least meet and talk about this?"

I'd ignored her and treated her messages with the contempt they deserved.

I texted her a few times when I was drunk... but they were largely insulting messages; questioning everything from her moral fibre to her intellectual capacity. I regretted sending them, not because I'd been rude, but because it gave her the impression that I was still angry about her. Which I'm not.

She used to say this funny thing when we argued, when I got angry and shouted at her. She said she quite liked it because it showed that I cared. I wasn't generally one for affection, or compliments, and I preferred to sleep without half her body draped over mine, as a rule. She used to compare me to our dog – Eric – because I changed my expression about as often as Eric changed his.

I even saw her once, further down the aisle in a local supermarket. Fortunately, she had her back to me so she didn't see me. I hid by the multipack crisps until she'd gone.

"I want to see you."

"Why?"

"I'm ill."

"I'm not a doctor."

"Please come. I need to see you."

"I'm not coming."

I went. But only because she sounded weird on the phone.

"Bloody hell."

When I had last seen my wife (ex-wife) in that supermarket, I'd felt a deep pang somewhere inside of me. It hit me like a brick. It was a physical pain and, for a moment, I thought I was going to be sick. I held it in and scuttled off to my hiding place amongst the crisps. I was there for quite a while, waiting for my heart to stop thumping and my palms to stop sweating. In the days that followed I put the whole thing down to some manifestation of sexual frustration. Lust. She had always been a good-looking woman. I only saw her from behind but her hair was as lustrous as ever and her figure... well, she even looked sexy pushing a shopping trolley.

It was one of the reasons I was determined not to see her... knowing that I wouldn't be able to resist jumping into bed with her if she even so much as touched my hand.

Since the break-up I hadn't... done anything with anyone else. Tried not to think about it. Just concentrated on work and not on her unbelievable body and the things she used to do to me in the bedroom.

That thought was in my mind as I knocked on her door. The touch of her hand had the same effect on me that one touch of Mountbank's hairy hand had on others.

"Don't be a fool, Dodd."

But then I saw her.

When I was younger, I had a friend who dabbled with drugs. Before I went off to university he was just a normal looking lad, fresh faced and ruddy cheeked with the lovely unlined skin that kids take for granted. But when I saw him again... it was like he had aged fifty years in one. Thin hair, ravaged teeth, battle scarred face. Heroin apparently, followed by some similarly destructive stuff designed to ease him off. Dispensed by the local pharmacist. Heroin had robbed him of his youth and his vitality, of his teeth and his complexion. I didn't recognise him at first... he looked like an old hag.

My wife had a similar look, emaciated and hollow, skeletal and malnourished... but it wasn't heroin that had battered her and beaten her and broken her down... but cancer.

"You daft cow... why didn't you tell me?"

## Chapter 12

# Disciplined and self-controlled outside, you tend to be worrisome and insecure inside

"Mr Dodd... Alistair... are you alright?"

Mountbank was looking at me, rather than at the inside of his own eyelids. It was rare for Mountbank to have his eyes open in between consultations. The effort of doling out his marginal gains seemed to drain him, although I often noted that he found the attractive young ladies more draining than the old, balding men. The previous consultation should have cleaned him out. An extremely lithe and flexible woman had requested a smidgeon more balance, for the sake of her ballet. It was only a hobby, she said, but she did take it very seriously. She had a relentless desire for perfection, so she said. Mountbank had charged her £1,000 and placed his hands over her ears... for it is the canal that controls our sensation of dizziness. I would have put money on him putting his hands on her stomach or on her hips... but he restrained himself. And he remembered to ask for permission this time. I think... I hadn't been paying that much attention.

"I wonder if I could have a word with you at some point, in private?" I asked, surprising myself as I did. I didn't even know I wanted a word with him in private.

Ogden glanced up from his phone.

"Whatever you want to ask you can ask in front of me," he said with that easy belligerence of his that made you want to throw something at him.

"It's private," I said.

"Even better," Ogden said. He was the kind of guy who didn't pronounce his Ts making the word "better" sound like it only had one syllable. "I'm all ears."

"Perhaps we can speak later," I said to Mountbank.

But, once more, Ogden answered. "No time like the present."

Mountbank just looked at me expectantly with his big, docile eyes.

I wanted to shake him for letting Ogden dominate him so completely. Why couldn't the bloody man speak for himself? It was like watching a game of Simon Says. Ogden says this. Ogden says that. Buy a house. Stay beyond five. Don't speak to journalists.

I'd make him speak.

"I wanted to ask you about your time in the church."

I hadn't wanted to.

"Hang on, sunshine..." began Ogden, but I ignored him.

"I'm not clear... did you leave of your own volition because you felt you'd transcended the teachings of the church or did they kick you out for being a heretic?"

"He's not going to answer that," said Ogden. "And we need to have words, sunshine."

"I've had enough words from you... and if you call me sunshine one more time..."

"Peace, gentlemen."

Mountbank's quiet voice restored order.

"I'll answer the question."

Ogden and I were staring at each other, like rutting stags. I was willing him to say something... anything... and I would have gone for him. Sod the book. Bugger the substantial advance. To hell with what my editor might say about it. The satisfaction of punching Ogden in the face would be my legacy; something I could tell the grandkids about. Cancer-faking, ex-wife shagging all round dickhead. "Yes children, I smacked him right in the mouth." *Go on, just one more word.* But after a moment or two, he took his phone out of his pocket and returned his attention to that.

Mountbank waited until I returned my attention to him.

"It took me a long time to properly identify my giftings," said Mountbank in response to the question I hadn't even wanted to ask. "For many years I just assumed I had the gift of healing. Many people have, it's entirely biblical. We would see miracles, Mr Dodd, real miracles. Lives changed. Illnesses bested. Peace restored. But as time went on, I just started to realise that it was me... my power... not the power of God... not the power of prayer or the use of anointing oils... just me. I could feel it, somewhere within my body. The power was coming from my soul. And once I'd realised that, well, there wasn't much room for me in the church anymore."

"So, they did kick you out?"

I was starting to sound as belligerent as Ogden.

"I'd prefer to say it was a mutual decision."

I had spoken to some of the Church Elders, those who had served with Tony Griffiths for many years, and they were definitely of the opinion that it was not a mutual decision. They'd used phrases like "false prophet" and "wolf in sheep's clothing." They had even hinted at some allegations of sexual impropriety.

"Is that when you changed your name?"

"Yes," said Mountbank simply. "I felt it was right."

"Like a stage name?"

"Not as such... more of a delineation point. A line in the sand."

"But why that name?"

Ogden cocked his ear once more. He probably didn't even realise the meaning of the name.

"Because belief must sometimes go beyond reason."

Mountbank was still looking at me with his big wet eyes. I noticed, for the first time, that he didn't really blink. I got a sense of what it must have been like to be treated by him... that unflinchingly bland stare. The eyes, once they were on you, stayed on you. Like the eyes of a painting that seem to follow you around the room, they just gave me an uneasy feeling.

I wrote something down, just to break eye contact.

"Is there anything else?" asked Mountbank. "You seem troubled."

Ogden continued to watch.

The very thought of mentioning my wife (ex-wife) in Ogden's presence made me feel physically sick.

"No," I said. "Nothing you can help with anyway."

## Chapter 13

# At times you are extroverted, affable, sociable, while at other times you are introverted, wary, reserved

Bloody idiotic stupid woman. Idiot bloody infuriating woman. Stubborn stupid idiotic stupid woman. Mad, stubborn, self-sufficient, martyr of a bloody woman.

"What are you thinking?" asked my wife.

I hadn't realised she'd woken. I was sitting in an armchair as she slept. Neither of us had moved in about five hours. I was just staring out of the window, although there wasn't much to see. I could see the top of a few other houses but I'd seen them before... when I had lived in that house. With her. My wife. Before.

I had a notepad on my lap and had told her, quite unconvincingly, that I could work whilst she slept. I was supposed to be etching out the broad structure for the chapter about Mountbank and his eviction from the church. At least I had something fresh to offer on that... the Messianic confession that Mountbank had given me. The healing in his hands. That should sell a few copies. Everyone loves a heretic.

But my page was blank. I'd just been staring. I could have been staring anywhere, but it just so happened there was a window in front of my eyes. I wondered how long she had been watching me, and whether she saw my lips moving. Bloody, stubborn woman... why didn't she call earlier?

"Nothing really," I said.

"You're angry with me," she said.

She always could read me.

"Yes, I am. If only you'd come to me earlier..."

"We've been through it," she said.

We had. There was nothing I could do. There was nothing they could do. She was infested. I knew it, she'd told me, but I let her tell me again. The first opinion and the second opinion had concurred. I wanted a third opinion, just to be bloody minded if nothing else, but my mother-in-law forbade it.

"What about America? We can go there... they have special treatments there. Lasers and all that."

"She's been through enough," my mother-in-law said. "Don't you think we've thought of everything while you've been in hiding?"

"It is what it is," said my wife.

She sounded tired. Doubly tired. Her body was wasting away. Sometimes I sat there, watching her sleep, and I swear I could see her visibly decaying... her skin melting into the mattress, her bones being absorbed into the duvet. She was rotting away, but rotting alive.

She was also tired because I was acting like a toddler, saying the same things over and over and over and waiting for her to say the same things in response – even though nothing could change and we had both said everything we needed to say.

Or apparently not.

"I'm sorry," she said.

"Don't be sorry. I'm being an idiot. Just angry. Not at you. Just at this."

"I didn't mean that. I mean I'm sorry... about what happened."

What Happened. That Thing. The Mistake. The Lapse in Judgement. I don't think we'd ever openly said what "that thing" was. Shagging Ogden.

And Ogden? Anyone but him.

It never made sense to me... why she would somehow fall into bed with Ogden. I was bolshy... so why not someone gentle? I was opinionated... so why not someone inoffensive? I was inattentive... so why not someone caring? I was complacent... so why not someone romantic? If she had gone to bed with my opposite, I could, on some level, have understood it. It would have made sense. But she hadn't. She'd gone to bed with another version of me... but a worse version.

"I don't know why I did it," she said in her weak little voice, as if she had read my mind, "I can't explain it, not even to myself... but I always loved you. Still do."

There was so much I should have said there... don't worry, it was my fault really, I was working too hard, I took you for granted, I was withdrawn, I let you down, I was no angel, I had some friends you didn't know about, I should have tried harder, I should have shown you some attention... but I didn't because... I don't know why, I just didn't.

I should probably have said that I loved her too.

But I didn't because I've never been able to do that kind of thing. I just stay in my box. My stupid, narrow-minded, enclosed, solid little box. I'm an idiot.

Something my mum said came back to me, "there's more to this life than can be measured with a ruler." As I looked at my putrefying wife, I realised she might be right.

"Are you up for a little drive?" I asked.

## Chapter 14

# You have a great need for other people to like and admire you

"But it's after five..." said Mountbank, as I eased my wife as gently as I could into the chair opposite him.

Mountbank looked at my wife; her pallid face, her wasted frame, and then glanced at his watch. Even his half-closed, bloodshot eyes could see that the woman slumped in the chair opposite him was half-dead. But Mountbank didn't see anyone or anything after five.

Mountbank looked to Ogden for support; surely this was no cash cow. Ogden gave no response whatsoever.

"It's after five," he said again.

"I'm sorry dear, I did try to stop them..."

Mrs Mountbank was at the back of the room, still holding on to the handle of the door which she had been compelled to open simply due to the weight of my insistent body.

Adam, fortunately, hadn't intervened.

"We don't see anyone after five," said Mountbank again.

He sounded pathetic, still seated in his padded chair, opposite my decaying wife. I wanted to shake him for being so weak and insipid. I wanted to throttle him until his gentle little voice turned into a scream of pain, or anything that might resemble a real human emotion. I wanted to punch him for being so heartless – a girl on the verge of death sitting opposite him – and all he wanted to do was go home and have a cheap little dinner in his stupid little kitchen.

"Maybe just this once," said Ogden, before he turned on his heel and left the room.

On the drive over, the one thing I couldn't get out of my mind was the worry that Ogden might suddenly become instantly attracted to my wife once again. And vice versa. That they'd leap on each other, falling instantly in love and lust once more. I obsessed over it, mile by mile. It didn't matter that my wife was asleep, huddled inside a huge coat, with not even enough energy to close her own car door. It didn't matter that she looked like a smack addict. It didn't matter that she was visibly dying. In my mind's eye she was still beautiful and I wouldn't have put it past Ogden to try it on with anyone. But, except for one very quick glance, Ogden hadn't even looked at her. In fact, he'd looked anywhere but at her. It ate away at me, nonetheless, until he buggered off.

That wasn't the only thing that ate away at me either. The whole stupid idea ate away at me. What was I thinking? What was I doing? "Well, if this doesn't work," I muttered to myself sarcastically as I drove along, "I'll try some voodoo or maybe get some nice herbs from a Chinese doctor. Maybe a foot massage will do the business."

But then I'd looked across at my wife, slumped in the passenger seat, and I just couldn't help myself.

So, there I was.

Idiot.

"I'd like you to give her a consultation please," I said after Ogden had left. "Please."

Mountbank looked at me for what seemed like a long time. That stare again.

"Why?" he said, eventually.

"What do you mean, why?"

I pointed at my wife – my desiccated wife. That is why, you goddamn fool. Open your bloody eyes.

"You don't believe in me. You think I'm a fraud."

There was no point denying it.

"Yes."

"Isn't that what you're going to say in your book?"

"Yes."

"Then why? Why bring her to me?"

Again, I looked at my wife, but I didn't see her. Not as a deflated wreck of a human being anyway. I saw a vision of how she used to be when we first met at university. Tight jeans and tighter tops. A drink always in her hand. Flirting with everyone, even girls. Opinionated in seminars, even more opinionated at the bar. The ability to look good, even with a hangover. I saw her on our wedding day, looking unbelievable, getting up to do a speech which turned out to be much better than mine. I saw her on the day we brought Eric home, our dog. The way she fussed and cuddled him and then called him a cheeky little bugger for doing his business on a new rug. I saw her with tears in her eyes, watching a film. I saw her reading a book, tossing it aside because it was terrible. I saw her drinking a cup of tea because...

I just saw her.

"People come here because they're desperate. Well, I'm desperate. I'll try anything."

Mountbank did that thinking thing.

"And what would you have me do?" asked Mountbank, after a while.

"Ali, let's go," said the emaciated shape that was once my wife, "he can't do anything. He's a fraud. And one per cent won't do me any good anyway."

Her voice sounded far away.

"He can do more than one per cent. He can do anything. He's Archibald Mountbank."

"How do you know that?" asked Mountbank, looking ever so slightly surprised.

"Ogden told me."

"Ogden is a liar," said Mrs Mountbank from the back of the room.

I turned to face her.

"I know. But I believe him... this once. I want your husband to give her whatever it takes…"

"My husband is Tony Griffiths."

"Well, Archibald Mountbank then."

"No," said Mrs Mountbank. "He'll die." No histrionics, no drama. Just "he'll die."

"If he doesn't… she will." I turned back to Mountbank. "Didn't you do the same for Ogden?"

"Is that what he told you?" asked Veronica.

"Yes. And I want the same. Or, she does. Ten per cent, twenty per cent, whatever she needs."

"It's just not possible," said Mrs Mountbank, her voice starting to fray a little now. "I apologise to your wife, but he can't save everyone."

"Ali, let's go," said that far away voice.

"No. Mountbank, please. I'm desperate."

I don't know why I expected anything. She didn't have a ticket. It was after five. She didn't have big breasts. She was just another case to him, another revenue stream, another appointment as he headed towards retirement. But I found myself praying. "Please God, make him treat her."

How ridiculous – praying to a god that I don't believe in, pleading with him to compel another fraud to do something that I didn't believe in either. I was the worst kind of idiot. But my wife…

Mountbank peered around me so he could see his wife. Mr and Mrs Mountbank stared at each other. I glanced from one to the other, but couldn't see anything passing between them… except for that intense, unblinking stare.

After what seemed like a lifetime, Mrs Mountbank turned on her heel and left the room. She closed the door gently behind her. Mountbank sighed and I wondered if I could see tears in his eyes.

"If I am to do this…" he said, "I need you to believe."

I swallowed… everything – my pride, my credulity, my

intellect... everything.

So, Adam Durlitz was right after all.

"I believe."

"In which case, I will need permission to place my hands on your wife's stomach. I do not mean to suggest that the cancer is concentrated within the stomach but as an approximation..."

Postscript – she lived.

Mountbank died three months later.

Mrs Mountbank returned to her former name, Veronica Griffiths, her former home and her former church. She wouldn't speak to me again.

Ogden...? Who cares?

# About the author

G.A. Milnthorpe is an internationally best-selling author, albeit without the "best". He is a Yorkshireman by birth and inclination, but a southerner by location. He is married with two children and a dog.

You can find him on Twitter, Goodreads and other random places.

ROUNDFIRE
BOOKS

# FICTION

Put simply, we publish great stories. Whether it's literary or popular, a gentle tale or a pulsating thriller, the connecting theme in all Roundfire fiction titles is that once you pick them up you won't want to put them down.

If you have enjoyed this book, why not tell other readers by posting a review on your preferred book site.

Recent bestsellers from Roundfire are:

### The Bookseller's Sonnets

Andi Rosenthal

*The Bookseller's Sonnets* intertwines three love stories with a tale of religious identity and mystery spanning five hundred years and three countries.

Paperback: 978-1-84694-342-3 ebook: 978-184694-626-4

### Birds of the Nile

An Egyptian Adventure

N.E. David

Ex-diplomat Michael Blake wanted a quiet birding trip up the Nile – he wasn't expecting a revolution.

Paperback: 978-1-78279-158-4 ebook: 978-1-78279-157-7

**Blood Profit$**
The Lithium Conspiracy
J. Victor Tomaszek, James N. Patrick, Sr.
The blood of the many for the profits of the few… *Blood Profit$* will
take you into the cigar-smoke-filled room where American policy
and laws are really made.
Paperback: 978-1-78279-483-7 ebook: 978-1-78279-277-2


**The Burden**
A Family Saga
N.E. David
Frank will do anything to keep his mother and father apart. But
he's carrying baggage – and it might just weigh him down …
Paperback: 978-1-78279-936-8 ebook: 978-1-78279-937-5


**The Cause**
Roderick Vincent
The second American Revolution will be a fire lit from an internal
spark.
Paperback: 978-1-78279-763-0 ebook: 978-1-78279-762-3


**Don't Drink and Fly**
The Story of Bernice O'Hanlon: Part One
Cathie Devitt
Bernice is a witch living in Glasgow. She loses her way in her
life and wanders off the beaten track looking for the garden of
enlightenment.
Paperback: 978-1-78279-016-7 ebook: 978-1-78279-015-0

## Gag
Melissa Unger
One rainy afternoon in a Brooklyn diner, Peter Howland punctures
an egg with his fork. Repulsed, Peter pushes the plate away and
never eats again.
Paperback: 978-1-78279-564-3 ebook: 978-1-78279-563-6


## The Master Yeshua
The Undiscovered Gospel of Joseph
Joyce Luck
Jesus is not who you think he is. The year is 75 CE. Joseph ben Jude
is frail and ailing, but he has a prophecy to fulfil ...
Paperback: 978-1-78279-974-0 ebook: 978-1-78279-975-7


## On the Far Side, There's a Boy
Paula Coston
Martine Haslett, a thirty-something 1980s woman, plays hard on
the fringes of the London drag club scene until one night which
prompts her to sign up to a charity. She writes to a young Sri
Lankan boy, with consequences far and long.
Paperback: 978-1-78279-574-2 ebook: 978-1-78279-573-5


## Tuareg
Alberto Vazquez-Figueroa
With over 5 million copies sold worldwide, *Tuareg* is a classic
adventure story from best-selling author Alberto Vazquez-
Figueroa, about honour, revenge and a clash of cultures.
Paperback: 978-1-84694-192-4

Readers of ebooks can buy or view any of these bestsellers by clicking on the live link in the title. Most titles are published in paperback and as an ebook. Paperbacks are available in traditional bookshops. Both print and ebook formats are available online.

Find more titles and sign up to our readers' newsletter at
http://www.johnhuntpublishing.com/fiction

Follow us on Facebook at https://www.facebook.com/JHPfiction
and Twitter at https://twitter.com/JHPFiction